To George, the most wonderful boy in the world. You are such a kind and gentle soul, and the world is a happier place with you in it. Thank you for being the wonderful, beautiful, inspiring boy you are. Love you lots, Momma Zo xxx – Z.A.

For George, who is true to himself even in a world full of judgement and boxes. For Molly, who is full of love for her brother, and fierce in the face of adversity. Keep being yourselves. I love you always and forever – K.A.

For my brother and sister, love you both so much xx – T.O'B.

My Brother George is a uclanpublishing book

First published in Great Britain in 2023 by
uclanpublishing
University of Central Lancashire
Preston, PR1 2HE, UK

Text copyright © Kelly & Zoey Allen, 2023
Illustrations copyright © Tara O'Brien, 2023

978-1-915235-39-8

1 3 5 7 9 10 8 6 4 2

The right of Kelly & Zoey Allen and Tara O'Brien to be identified
as the authors and illustrator of this work respectively has been asserted
in accordance with the Copyright, Designs and Patents Act 1988.

A CIP catalogue record for this book is available from the British Library.

Printed and bound in Great Britain by Page Bros Group.

MY BROTHER GEORGE

KELLY & ZOEY ALLEN
ILLUSTRATED BY TARA O'BRIEN

uclanpublishing

This is *me*.
This is my *family*.

My name is Molly.
I have curly hair, big blue
eyes, and I *love* to sing.

This is my *brother*, George. He has beautiful long hair, bright hazel eyes, and the *best* laugh.

He's a *teeny* bit older than me, but we play together *all* the time.

He tells *funny* jokes and he calls himself the Dog Whisperer.

He loves all dogs, even the *really* big ones! I think he's so *brave*.

Our *favourite* days together are full of adventure.

We *love* to climb trees,

search for bugs,

Throw sticks for Ziggy, and *stomp* in muddy puddles.

We go to the beach to chase the salty waves and feel the sand between our toes. We build sandcastles, slurp on ice cream, and *giggle* until our bellies hurt.

Then, when we go home, we *snuggle* on the sofa
in our PJs and drink hot chocolate.

Our *least* favourite days are full of boring chores and early bedtimes.

TOYS!

We don't like brushing our hair . . .

. . . or poop-scooping!

And we REALLY *don't like it* when people call George a girl.

When he was little, he'd wear *pretty* clips in his hair,
long beads around his neck, and *cute, cosy* cardigans.

Other children would *laugh* at him, but I always thought he looked *cool*.

He doesn't wear them *any more*, but he still has *lovely* long hair. This *confuses* some people. I'm not sure why.

They call him a *girl* and
think he's my *sister*.

They touch his hair
and they think his
favourite colour
is *pink*.

I haven't always been able to stick up for him, but now I'm *older*,
I feel *brave enough* to tell people he's my *brother*.

They usually apologise, they always blush,
and sometimes they even *ignore* me.

One time, a lady said he was *too pretty* to be a boy.
This made me *angry* and I didn't know what to say . . .

But George *did*.

I think you should *get to know someone* before finding out their gender.

And it made me *smile*.

Ever since, George has grown *braver* and *stronger*.

He plays with my dolls.
He sometimes plaits his hair.

Sometimes he wears
my clothes.

He doesn't like football. He loves zombies, and baking cakes.

His favourite colour is *red* (not pink)
and he's *really good* at painting nails.

People still call him a *girl*,
Sometimes children *laugh* at him.

But, he's no longer afraid to be
who he wants to be.

So when people call him a *girl*
or *laugh* at him, he doesn't get sad.

Instead, he tries to help them *understand*.
And I'm there, by his side, in case he *needs* me.

This is my brother, George. He's cool, he's funny, and he has *beautiful* long hair.

I love my brother George, and I'll *always* be there for him, *no matter what.*